THE
Best Ballerina

BONNEY PRESS

Published by Bonney Press,
an imprint of Hinkler Books Pty Ltd
45-55 Fairchild Street
Heatherton Victoria 3202 Australia
www.hinkler.com.au

BONNEY
PRESS

© Hinkler Books Pty Ltd 2014, 2015

Author: Melissa Mattox
Illustrator: Irisz Agócs

ISBN: 978 1 7436 7798 8

Printed and bound in China

To Rowan - MM

THE Best Ballerina

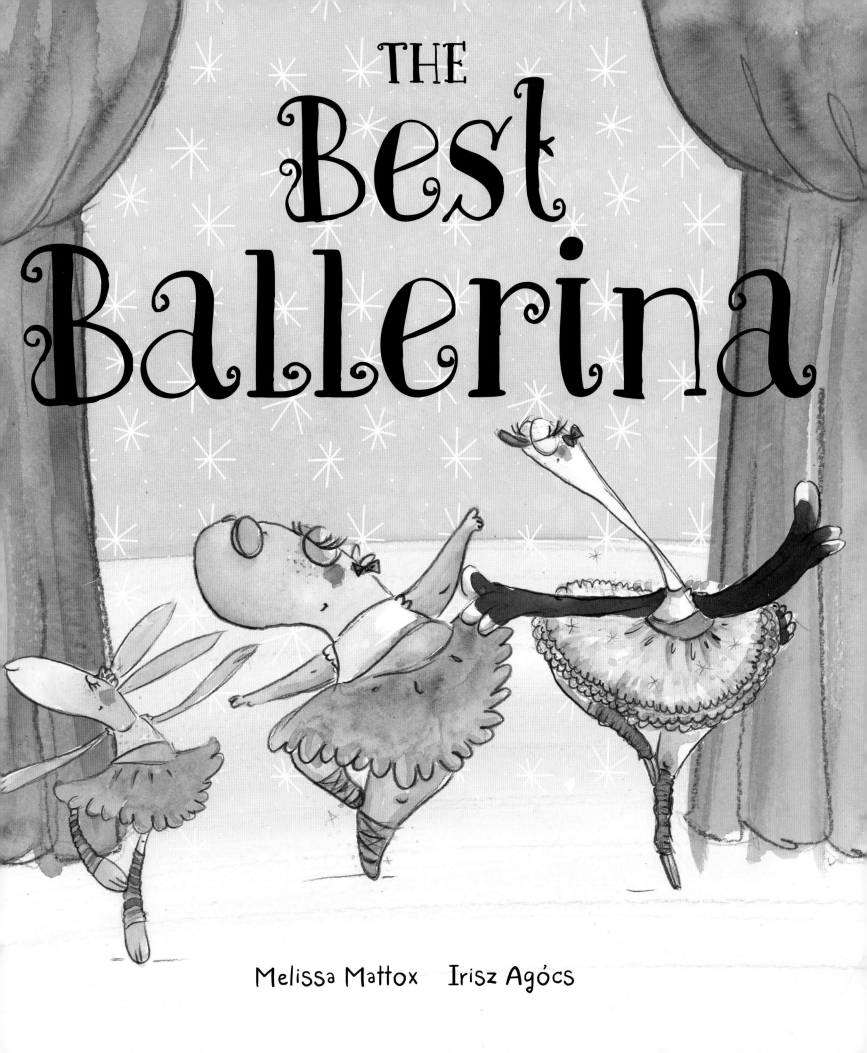

Melissa Mattox   Irisz Agócs

Harriet was so excited. She wanted to show her friends her new ballet slippers.

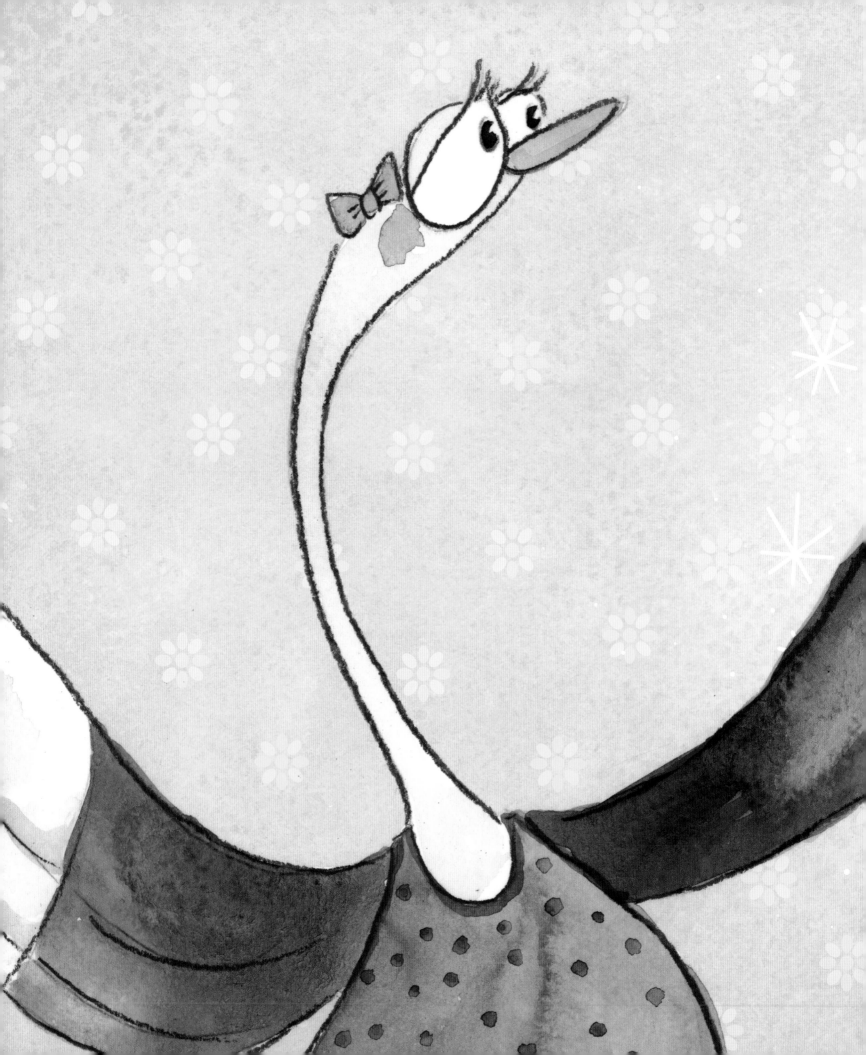

"Those are beautiful! And they match my tutu perfectly," said Olivia. "Together they will make a perfect fairy-princess costume."

"Not without this, they don't!" said Rachel.

"Ooooh," hummed the girls, happily.

The three friends twirled and spun, leaped and pirouetted.

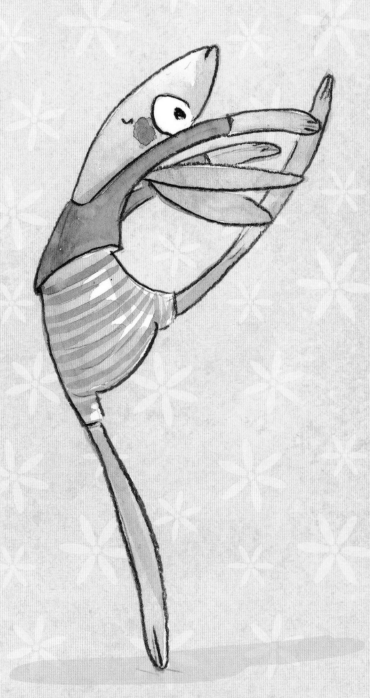

As they danced, all they could think about was the upcoming big ballet recital.

"Oh no! I just realised something," said Harriet, stopping mid-dance. "We only have enough pieces for one fairy-princess costume.

Only one of us can dance in the big ballet recital!"

"Well, it should be me," said Olivia.
"I have the longest legs."

"But I brought the tiara!" interrupted Rachel.

"That shouldn't matter!"
cried Harriet.

Each girl tried on the costume.

But no matter how hard they tried, it just didn't look right.

The friends continued to argue, each one convinced
that she was the best fairy-princess dancer.

"Ladies, why all the fussing?" asked Madam Hoot.

Harriet, Olivia, and Rachel explained the problem.

Madam Hoot listened carefully.

"The night sky is never lit by just one star but shines because there are many," she said. "Why don't you three get some rest? Tomorrow you can choose who should wear the costume at the recital."

That night the girls lay in their beds, staring up at the dark night sky, all lit up with hundreds of twinkling starry lights.

The next morning, the three friends met before the dance.

"I'm sorry we fought," said Rachel. "I think Harriet should dance. She has the best twirls."

"But Olivia has the best plies," said Harriet.

"No one can beat Rachel's leaps,"
offered Olivia.

A crowd had gathered to watch the girls perform.
"Bravo!" "Hooray!" "Magnificent!" they shouted.

"I think the best fairy princess for the big ballet recital should be ... all three of us!" said Olivia. "Together we make true fairy-princess magic!"